This book ~~belongs to:~~
is shared with

_____

_____

_____

the fish who searched for water

to all who seek

© 2016 Conscious Stories LLC

Illustrations by Marcel Marais

Published by
Conscious Stories LLC
4800 Baseline Rd.
Suite E104-365
Boulder, CO
80303
USA

www.consciousstories.com

First Edition
Library of Congress
Control Number: 2017901958
ISBN 978-1-943750-07-8

Printed in China

1 2 3 4 5 6 7 8 9 10

The last 20 minutes of every day are precious.

Dear parents, teachers, and readers,

This story has been gift-wrapped with two simple mindfulness practices to help you connect more deeply with your children in the last 20 minutes of each day.

● Quietly set your intention for calm, open connection.

● Then start your story time with the **Snuggle Breathing Meditation**. Read each line aloud and take slow, deep breaths together in order to relax and be present.

● At the end of the story, you will find **The Love Hunt**. The questions help your children know that they are surrounded by love wherever they are, which is the moral of our story. Have fun finding love together.

Enjoy snuggling into togetherness!

Andrew

Snuggle Breathing

Our story begins with us breathing together.
Say each line aloud and then
take a slow deep breath in and out.

I breathe for me

I breathe for you

I breathe for us

I breathe for all that surrounds us

Once upon a time,
there was a little fish

Who never felt at home,
he had a special wish.

He dreamed of finding water,
enough to quench his soul,

to take away his loneliness,
and make his pieces whole.

"Where, oh where, is water?"
sought the little fish.
"I will shrivel up if I can't fulfill this wish."

"Is it here?"

"Or here?"

"Maybe here?"

9

No one had the answers
that he'd believe or trust,

so onward he went swimming,
thinking that he must.

He swam...

And swam...

and swam.

15

He paused at a few places
to have a little sip,

finding some refreshment
on his tiresome trip.

On he swam,
thirsty for more.
What he had found
couldn't be all.

One day he leapt up in the air.

It was brave and bold
and done on a dare.

He thought,
"If I can get the view of a bird

I'll soon find water,"
or so he had heard.

He leapt in the air,
took a great big gasp,

but his gills shut down,
drowned with the blast.

Thankfully gravity pulled him back in
to where he could breathe
and where he could swim.

He nearly drowned
with all the fresh air.

It was empty of something
that offered fish care.

It was empty of fluid
and flow and delight.

It was empty of water!!
That shook the fish right.

24

The water I seek
surrounds me right now.
Somehow it seems it's inside me.

OH WOW!

I don't need to swim
or to seek or to look

to discover the water
I simply mistook.

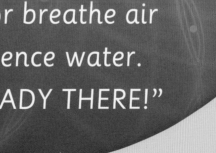

I don't need to struggle
or quest or breathe air
to experience water.
IT'S ALREADY THERE!"

Where did you find love today?

We all search for love in our own way. Sometimes we find love but don't recognize it: Sometimes, love is too close to see.

Answer the questions in **The Love Hunt** and enjoy a moment together.

Count your blessings

The Love Hunt

1

Where did you look for love today?

2

Who showed you love today?

3

When did you forget love today?

4 What helped you remember love?

5 How did you love yourself today?

6 Who did you show love to today?

7 Do you need more love before going to sleep?

8 Sweet dreams

29

the collection

The Conscious Bedtime Story Club

snuggling into togetherness

the fish who searched for water

the prayer who searched for God

Andrew Newman
Illustrated by Alexis Aronson

the bee who could not choose her flower

Andrew Newman
Illustrated by Marcella Murad

the dad who didn't know

the hug who got stuck

Andrew

the forgetful elephant

Andrew Newman
Illustrated by

the laughing witch

Andrew Newman

a little light

Andrew Newman
Illustrated by Rocío Beljuví

the elephant who tried to tiptoe

how diablo became Spirit

Andrew Newman
& Anna Breytenbach
Illustrated by Alexis Aronson

the boy who searched for silence

Andrew Newman
Illustrated by Alexis Aronson

the tree of goodness

Andrew Newman
Illustrated by Marcella Murad

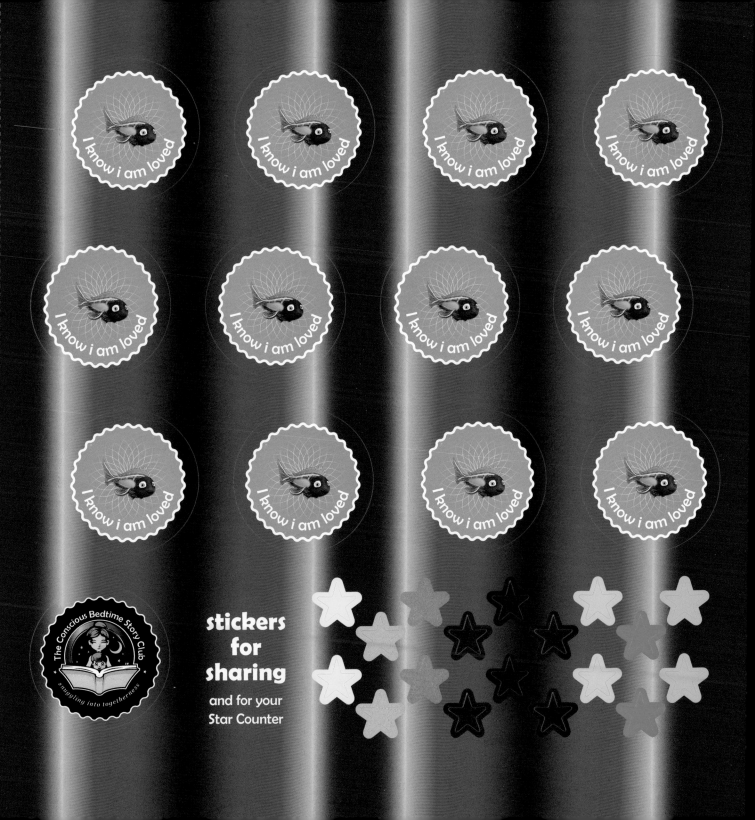

I know i am loved

The Conscious Bedtime Story Club

snuggling into togetherness

stickers for sharing

and for your Star Counter

Star Counter

Every time you breathe together and
read aloud, you make a star shine in the
night sky.

Place a sticker, or color in a star, to count
how many times you have read this book.